This book belongs to

_____

For Fred: the one I love.
—T.S.

For my Grandma and Grandpa Champion.
—A.B.

Library of Congress Cataloging-in-Publication Data is available.

2 4 6 8 10 9 7 5 3 1

Published by Sterling Publishing Co., Inc. 387 Park Avenue South, New York, NY 10016

Text copyright © 2005 by Teddy Slater
Illustrations copyright © 2005 by Aaron Boyd

Designed and produced for Sterling by COLOR-BRIDGE BOOKS, LLC, Brooklyn, NY

Distributed in Canada by Sterling Publishing
c/o Canadian Manda Group, 165 Dufferin Street
Toronto, Ontario, Canada M6K 3H6
Distributed in Great Britain and Europe by Chris Lloyd at Orca Book Services,
Stanley House, Fleets Lane, Poole BH15 3AJ, England
Distributed in Australia by Capricorn Link (Australia) Pty. Ltd.
P.O. Box 704, Windsor, NSW 2756, Australia

Printed in China
All rights reserved

Sterling ISBN 1-4027-1986-8

Pigs in Love

by Teddy Slater • Illustrated by Aaron Boyd

Sterling Publishing Co., Inc.
New York

Pretty pink pigs on Valentine's Day,
all dressed up, with something to say.

They say it with flowers.

They say it with hearts.

They say it with candy
and strawberry tarts.

They say it to
their fathers.

They say it to
their mothers.

Sometimes they even say it
to their pesky little brothers.

Some say it to
a sweetheart.

Some say it to a buddy.

Some say it when they're all spruced up.

Some say it when they're muddy.

Some whisper in a loved one's ear.

Some even shout it—
loud and clear!

You can say it with a song.

You can say it with a poem.

You can say it at the playground.

You can say it in your home.

Sows and piglets, hogs, and swine—
everyone's someone's valentine.

So join the fun
and choose a way
to say "I love you"
on Valentine's Day!